The Mystery of the Noises in the Attic

by Tracy Zimmerman

illustrated by Liz Callen

HOUGHTON MIFFLIN   BOSTON

It was a sunny Saturday morning. Brenda and her brother were cleaning up after their waffle breakfast. Brenda asked Mom if she could go for a bike ride with her friends.

"Not until this afternoon," Mom said. "Remember, we have to pick up your fundraising cookies today so that you can sell them next weekend with your girls' chorus."

"Cookies! Can we eat them?" asked Jeremy. Brenda's brother always got excited about food.

"No way!" cried Brenda, glaring at Jeremy. "As soon as we bring them home, they go straight into the attic."

"Only the ghost will eat them then," Jeremy said, disappointed.

"What ghost?" Brenda asked.

"You know—the ghost. Every attic has a ghost." Jeremy sounded serious. Brenda smiled at her brother's vivid imagination.

On Wednesday night, Mom was out at a meeting at school. Melissa, a twelfth-grader, was staying with Brenda and Jeremy. The girls were doing their homework in the kitchen when Jeremy ran through the doorway. He was breathing so hard he could hardly speak.

"Quick! Melissa! Brenda! Come up to my room! I heard a weird sound coming from the attic! It's a ghost, I just know it!" Jeremy cried.

Melissa leaped up from the table and followed Jeremy to the stairs. Brenda followed more slowly. *Jeremy has ghosts on his mind lately*, she thought. *He thinks any sound is a ghost.*

The three of them sat in Jeremy's room and waited. Nothing happened. "I heard something, honest I did," Jeremy said as they went back downstairs. "It was like a kid running across the ceiling."

The next night, Brenda was brushing her teeth when she thought she heard something overhead. She turned off the faucet and listened closely. There it was again! It was a scuffing sound, not a sound that the wind would make.

What could be making the sound? Brenda didn't believe in ghosts. Could she be wrong? She felt a sudden chill. Then she shook her head. *Jeremy is young enough to believe in ghosts, but I'm not*, she thought. She went to bed.

The next day was Friday. Brenda looked forward to selling cookies with her girls' chorus the following morning. That night she helped Jeremy put away a pile of clean clothes, chattering to him about the statewide competition that her chorus was entering. Suddenly, they both froze. Footsteps scurried overhead. Brenda and Jeremy looked at each other, then ran for the door.

"Mom!" they shouted together down the stairs. "Come quick!"

Soon, all of them crept up the stairs toward the attic. Mom went first, carrying a flashlight. Brenda and Jeremy followed close behind. As they neared the attic door, they heard a scratching sound coming from the other side. Mom turned around. "Are you ready for this?" she asked. Brenda and Jeremy nodded.

SANDWICH
COOKIES

Mom opened the door and shined the light inside.
Crumbs littered the floor. She swung the light around the
edges of the room. There! A pair of eyes glowed yellow
in the faint light. Brenda gasped.

Mom pulled a cord overhead, and the room flooded
with light. Against the wall crouched a raccoon!
Shredded boxes covered the floor. They were cookie
boxes.

"Kids, meet your ghost," Mom said.

Before Brenda or Jeremy could reply, the raccoon darted to the far end of the attic and disappeared in the corner. Mom followed it, her shoes crunching on cookie crumbs. "There's a hole over here in the corner. The raccoon must be able to climb up from the apple tree outside." Then she turned to them and laughed. "The raccoon likes cookies! Brenda, maybe it should join your girls' chorus!"